T0099709

OPERATION SAVE A GENERATION

By

Gloria Black

Order this book online at www.trafford.com
or email orders@trafford.com

Most Trafford titles are also available at major online book retailers.

© Copyright 2010 Gloria Black.
All rights reserved. No part of this publication may be reproduced, stored in a retrieval system,
or transmitted, in any form or by any means, electronic, mechanical, photocopying, recording,
or otherwise, without the written prior permission of the author.

The views expressed in this work are solely those of the author and do not necessarily reflect
the views of the publisher, and the publisher hereby disclaims any responsibility for them.

Printed in the United States of America.

ISBN: 978-1-4269-3426-1 (sc)
ISBN: 978-1-4269-3427-8 (e)

*Our mission is to efficiently provide the world's finest, most comprehensive book publishing
service, enabling every author to experience success. To find out how to publish your book,
your way, and have it available worldwide, visit us online at www.trafford.com*

Trafford rev. 8/28/2010

 www.trafford.com

North America & international
toll-free: 1 888 232 4444 (USA & Canada)
phone: 250 383 6864 ♦ fax: 812 355 4082

CHAPTER ONE

Blood and urine covered Samuel's jeans, and the outraged man continued to hold tight to his leg. Samuel screamed out from the pain in his thigh, but still he hung on to the fence for dear life. "Mom! Oh God! He keep screaming as the pain worsened. He began to wish through waterfalls of tears and pain that his mother were there. He wished he could get away, but most of all he wished the man would disappear. Samuel tried to move his injured thigh, but the overwhelming pain caused him to lose consciousness. Samuel's hands let go of the fence, and he leaned toward Gordy.

"Oh my God!," Gordy said out loud while letting go of the boy's leg in order to use both hands to support the boy's leaning limp body. On top of the bared wire fence Gordy saw the boy's jean covered thigh drenched in blood. The blood was flowing like a running faucet down the fence. Gordy braced his body against the fence and put an arm around the boy's lifeless shoulders. He reached his other hand under the boy's bleeding thigh, and lifted it up a little at a time. Finally the boy's thigh was dislodged from the sharp pointed metals of the fence. It wasn't an easy task for Gordy to keep the bleeding thigh in his hand while lifting the boy off the fence. The gash was deep, and the blood flowed down his hands, on to his clothes and shoes. "God please help me." Gordy prayed kneeling in the wild grass, inches from the fence with the boy in his arms. He knew a tourniquet was needed. He placed the boy on his side with the gash thigh on top. He balanced the boy by letting the back of him rest on his knees. Gordy quickly took off his jacket and removed his shirt. He put one end of the shirt between the boy's thighs, then tied both ends of the shirt together several times over the gash.

Gordy picked up his jacket, and took his cell phone from his jacket pocket first. Next he put one sleeve of the jacket between the boy's thigh and over the shirt. He then grabbed the other sleeve and tied the two sleeves tight over the gash. Big sweat beads rested on his eyelids before running down his face. With the phone in one hand, he leaned forward to placed two fingers on the boy's neck. He felt a small pulse. "Oh God please save the kid," he prayed as he dialed 911. With a bloody shaking hand he placed the phone to his ear.

A voice said, "911."

"Yes, I need an ambulance for a kid who's unconscious and he's lost a lot of blood."

The voice asked for an address.

"I don't know the address, because we've in a dead end alley way. But I'll run to the street to find out. It'll only take a few minutes," Gordy told the voice, and placed the phone down next to him. With care he moved his knees and gently rolled the boy on his back. He grabbed the phone, stood up, and ran like lighting out of the ally. The sun got brighter as he neared the street. "The alley is on Hills street," he told 911 after reading the street's name on the corner pole. Gordy stood in front of the alley and looked at the two boarded-up houses on each side of the alley. "The alley is 235, Hills street. It's between two boarded-up buildings." Gordy heard the voice give the address, and location for the ambulance. He hung up and ran back to kneel at the boy's side. He put his phone in his side pants side pocket, and leaned a little to take another pulse on the boy's neck. He felt a slight pulse again.

The boy looked to be eleven or twelve to Gordy. On the boy's ear was a small gleaming earing, and he wore designer sneakers which were blood stained. He felt sorry for the boy, yet he knew if the boy hadn't snatched his wallet none of this would have happened. Gordy heard the sirens. He got up, and ran out to signal them. On the street he could see the flashing lights. He jumped up and down, and waved his arms. The driver blew the loud ambulance horn to let Gordy know he saw him.

What appeared to have been a ghost street came alive with people when the ambulance stopped in front of the alleyway. Gordy lead the paramedics through the alley to where the boy laid. He stood back, and prayed as he watched the medics work fast on the boy. After seeing the medics give oxygen to the boy, Gordy saw them remove his bloody shirt and jacket from around the boy's thigh.

"Who made the tourniquets?" A medic asked, while several of them worked on the boy's thigh. Gordy stepped forward. His undershirt, pants, shoes, parts of his face and arms and hands were covered with dried and wet blood. The medics and other people in the alley stared at him. "Are you hurt?", a medic asked him.

"No," Gordy told the medic.

Minutes later, the boy was put on a stretcher, strapped in and taken out of the alley to the ambulance. Two officers, who were in the alley with the medics approached Gordy. After introducing themselves to him, they asked him for I.D.

My name is Gordy Mann. I don't have my wallet, because the kid snatched it and ran in this alley. He cut his leg on that fence," he said pointing to the fence. All that blood...and..."

"Take your time, we understand," The officer told Gordy as he prepared to write on his pad. Gordy felt tired, out of breath, and close to tears. He thought about smoking a cigarette, but remember he didn't smoke. He took a deep breath.

"Well..." Gordy said and licked his dry lips, then swallowed hard. The officers asked him if he needed some water. "Please, thank you," Gordy said. One Officer left the alley to get the water. Minutes later, the three were drinking ice cold spring water. Gordy drank most of his before continuing. Gordy noticed that just the three of them were in the alley. He felt better, and continued to tell what happened.

"It must have been about 2:30 or 3:00, this afternoon when I parked my cab on the empty parking lot across the street from Wenton Farms on Doat street. I saw a few kids around the store when crossing the street to the store. The door was opened. I went in. I played my numbers, then I took out my wallet." Gordy showed the officers by gesturing a step by step. "With my wallet in my hand I took out a ten dollar bill. I gave that to the store owner. He gave me my tickets and my change which I put in my wallet. I folded my wallet, reached to the back of my pocket to put it in, and that's when the kid from behind or to the side of me grabbed it.

"He ran out, and I ran after him." Gordy finished his water. "He ran down Doat street and turned up Hills to this alley. I kept yelling for him to take the money out and drop the wallet." Gordy looked at the two officers with a slight smile, "I do need my I.D.! Well anyway, he turned fast into this alley. He tried to climb that old barbed-wire fence," he said pointing to the blood stained fence. "But I ran up to the fence and grabbed his leg. He started kicking at me. I told him that I needed my I.D., too. I saw he had wet his jeans. He tried to put his other leg up and over the fence, but his thigh landed on the sharp ends of this barbed-wire." Gordy was at the fence. "He yelled so loud, it should have waken the dead. He yelled several times before he lost consciousness. I had to maneuver my body and his in order to dislodge his thigh from the fence." As Gordy demonstrated his moves, he happened to look down in the wild grass close to the other side of the fence. He kneeled down to get a closer look. He touched it.

"My luck just changed! Here is my wallet, but I'll have to go around the corner to get it." The officers came closer to the fence. The officer who had gotten the water said he would drive around the corner to retrieve the wallet. Within ten minutes, Gordy held his wallet in his hand. "Thank you," Gordy told the officer while he opened it and took out his I.D.'s, which he handed to the officer. The officer wrote down some information from the cards and smiled when he handed Gordy his I.D.'s back.

"I fell sorry for the boy and his parents. I would like to know who he is and meet his parents," Gordy told the officers during their walk out of the alley. One officer told him they were on their way to the store to ask questions. He gave Gordy an card where they could be reached, also the phone number of the General Hospital to inquire about the boy. Gordy thanked them, said his goodbys, and turned to walk up the street. Minutes later he heard a horn and a 911 pulled beside him. The officer who was driving told him to get in because they were going his way. Gordy smiled and got in. During the drive, one of the officers asked him if he could spare a few more minutes of his time by going into the store with them.

Gordy took a deep sigh, but told them he would. He looked at his cab across the street in the parking lot before the three entered the store.

All eyes were on them while they waited a few minutes for the store owner to clear the store and lock the door. When questioned, the store owner said he saw what had happened to Gordy and called 911. He gave the boy's description and the name Sammy, because he heard the kids call him that. They all thanked the owner for his time. Outside, officer Smith walked to the 911. Officer Green explained to Gordy that his partner was calling precinct twelve for a crime report.

"I'm going across the street to my cab, but I won't leave." Gordy said. Seconds later he unlocked the cab and got in. Gordy exhale. It felt good as he sat back to relax. He turned on the car and rolled down the windows. He took his phone from his pocket, and looked at it. No wonder he thought and turned the ranger back on. He placed his phone on its charger, looked at the two officers at their 911, leaned back, and closed his eyes. A noise woke him. Everything looked brighter when he opened his eyes. He saw both officers with smiles on their faces looking at him from outside his window. Gordy was tired and he had jumped a little. This made them smile.

Gordy was handed the report when he sat up. Both thanked him for being patient and told him it was a full report. They also told him that Samuel's mother was notified, and they were on their way to the hospital. Before they headed across the street, the two told him to get some rest. Gordy turned his engine on and proceeded home.

CHAPTER TWO

Seven and a half years left...boy oh boy! Can I do it without having a nervous breakdown? Sarah Willaby had started asking herself this question at least once a week. Samuel, who was going on thirteen and her only child, had became a hand full. She knew it wasn't unusual these days to be a single parent. She used to want her son to finish high school, go to college or trade school. Now she prayed for him to stay out of trouble, and to acknowledge God. She tried to keep him busy, but he kept making bad choices, and imitating past mistakes of others. It was Saturday. She worked part time at the restaurant through the week, full time on Saturdays, and some Sundays. Samuel went to the young center on Saturdays from 10:30 to 12:30. After that he had football practice from 1:00 to 4:00. Miss Mary, a kind and wise friend to Sarah lived upstairs. She looked after Samuel on Saturdays, from 10:00 in the morning till 6:00 or until Sarah arrived home. Miss Mary kept tabs on Samuel by calling the youth center, and his coach from time to time.

This Saturday was really busy at the restaurant, and she missed her call home time. Until her cell phone rang she had had no idea of the time. Her cell phone read 4:15, and the caller was the General Hospital. "Hello," Sarah said nervously, holding the phone tight to her ears. The lady's voice was kind as she greeted her and told her that Samuel was in the emergency room there. Sarah held her breath and continued to listen to her voice.

"He's stable, but he had to be given oxygen because he had lost consciousness and a great deal of blood from a deep gash on his thigh. Can you get here as soon as possible to sign permission papers for all procedures? Sarah felt her legs become weak. A dark dimension seem to engulf her. Her words seem to be choked. Then it was light again.

"Oh my God, I'm on my way! Thank you." Quickly she closed the cover to the phone. Some customers who had heard Sarah's voice, and then see her rush around the restaurant looked concerned. She dazedly got her belongings and told her employer why she had to leave. When She opened the restaurant door to leave, she heard voices in the back ground telling her to drive carefully and their prayers were with her.

On her way to her car Sarah used her cell phone to call Miss Mary. After hearing about Samuel, Miss Mary insisted she meet Sarah at the hospital. Sarah began praying for her son during her drive there. Halfway to the hospital her phone rang. It was the coach. She told him the reason her son didn't show up for practice. "I'm driving to the hospital now, I'll call you later. Thanks for calling me."

The coach reminded her how strong Samuel was, and he'll talk to her later.

Sarah parked in the emergency area, next to Miss Mary's small van. Miss Mary was at the front desk when Sarah walked through the emergency doors. Although Miss Mary smiled at her, she had noticed the tears in Miss Mary's eyes. The two embraced for a moment. Sarah had managed a smile when she asked the receptionist about Samuel Willaby. The receptionist asked Sarah to please follow her. Miss Mary waited in the waiting room. Sarah was led to a booth where she was asked questions about Samuel and handed papers to sign. The receptionist thanked Sarah and told her Samuel's room number.

Miss Mary saw Sarah coming and stood up. He's in room 22, Sarah told Miss Mary before they preceded down the hall to find it. Both of them couldn't help but notice how busy the rooms were. Finally they came to Samuel's room. The two entered. They saw Samuel's thigh wrapped and elevated with a pillow. Two bags hung on a stand. One bag had red liquid, the other contained white liquid and both were dripping the liquids through a tube into Samuel's arm. Samuel's eye's watered when he saw his mother's and Miss Mary's tears. Samuel looked tired and frighten. Sarah was speechless, and she felt a heaviness in her heart as she moved to her son's bedside. She placed her hand gently on his hand. Samuel closed his eyes, and tears ran down each side of his face. Miss Mary stood on the other side and watched a mother's love. Minutes later a doctor came in with Samuel's medical papers and pen. He introduced himself, and Sarah introduced herself and Miss Mary.

The doctor put on his glasses, while standing at the foot of the bed to read the report. When he was finished reading he asked Sarah if she knew how Samuel's thigh got cut. "No I don't doctor," she said.

The doctor looked at Samuel, who still had his eyes closed. He took off his glasses, and looked at Sarah. He asked her if she knew there was a police report.

Sarah looked bewildered as she answered,"No," while looking at her son first then Miss Mary back to the doctor. The doctor told her he would make a copy for her. Putting back on his glasses he wrote on the papers in his hands. Without looking up from writing the doctor told Sarah three things that were going to happen to Samuel. First, he would get stitches. Second, because he had lost a lot of blood and was unconscious when the ambulances brought him in, he needed to stay a few days for observation. Third a officer was coming to take a statement concerning what had happened today.

When the doctor finished reading and writing, he looked up to see a surprise look on Sarah's face. He told her not to worry. "When are you going to do the surgery?" Sarah asked him. He told her he'll be back in about a half of an hour to move him to the surgery room. "Can I hold his hand?" Sarah asked with pleading eyes. He smiled and shook his head to tell her no, and added that Samuel was going under anesthesia. Before going out of the door he told them the procedure should take about an hour.

"Thank you doctor," Sarah and Miss Mary said at the same time. The doctor closed the door behind him.

Sarah decided not to ask Samuel any questions until he felt better. Samuel's eyes were still closed. Miss Mary got up from the chair near the bed, and whispered something in Sarah's ear. Moments later the two joined hands at the foot of

Samuel's bed and prayed out loud. After prayer the two looked at Samuel's half closed slightly flicking eyes. Miss Mary looked at Sarah with a smile, but said nothing before she went back to the chair. Sarah moved to the stand beside her son. She bent to kiss him on the forehead and cheek. Moving her face to his ear she whispered she loved him, and told him not to be scared. The room was silent until a knock was heard, and two nurses came in. They were friendly with their greetings and busied themselves preparing Samuel and his bed for moving.

Samuel remained silent, and kept his eyes closed as he was rolled to the elevator by the two nurses. Sarah and Miss Mary followed, and got in the elevator when it came. Sarah kept an close eye on Samuel, but said nothing. Miss Mary squeezed Samuel's hand and told him she loved him before the elevator door opened on the surgery floor. They rolled him out of the elevator, and the two watched the nurses roll him to the surgery room. While waiting for the elevator Sarah turned to Miss Mary. "Samuel must have done something pretty bad. He didn't say a word, and he was peeping at everyone. Let's go and get the police report and read it in the cafeteria over coffee." Miss Mary agreed.

Sarah was silent while she and Miss Mary rode the elevator to the first floor.

Sarah and Miss Mary could see the main desk when the elevator door opened.

Within ten minutes Sarah was thanking the nurse at the desk for the police report.

She glanced at the report before folding it in half to put it in her purse. Once they had their coffee and were seated, Sarah took a few sips from the hot coffee before she took out the report.

"Miss Mary, please read this!" Sarah had almost forgot where she was at when she spoke a little too loud. "I'm sorry Miss Mary, I just can't believe what I just read.

Miss Mary put her coffee cup down, and took the report from Sarah. Sarah picked up her coffee cup and sipped on her coffee while Mary read the report. Miss Mary had tears in her eyes when she handed Sarah back the report and picked up her cup. Sarah opened her purse and took out her cell phone. "I've got to call Mr. Mann," she told Miss Mary, reading his number from the report and dialing it at the same time.

CHAPTER THREE

Gordy was lying on the couch trying to relax by watching a football game, but he keep thinking about Samuel Willaby. Gordy's phone rang. "Hello," Gordy said.

"Hello, is this Mr. Mann?"

"Yes it is."

"Mr. Mann, this is Sarah Willaby, I'm Samuel Willaby's mother. I'm calling to thank you for saving my son's life. Please forgive him for snatching your wallet." The tears began to run down Sarah's face.

"Thank you so much." Sarah sobbed.

"Ms. Willaby, I only did what needed to be done, but you're welcome. How is your son doing?"

"He's conscious, thank God, but he needed blood, and he's in surgery now receiving stitches. He'll be here for a few days."

"I'm very glad you called. I was going to call you later. Thank God, he's doing a lot better."

"Mr. Mann, would it be okay if we met in person when Samuel comes home?"

"Of course Ms. Willaby, I'll be looking forward to it."

"Good Mr. Mann, thank you and God bless you."

Gordy hung the phone up, but remained thinking about the conversation. A meeting with Samuel and his mother reminded him of so many other single mothers he had talked to at the school he taught at. Gordy wanted to be an inspirational mentor to children who were willing to listen to the power within themselves. He knew that if people, young or old, didn't listen to their conscience, the consequences of making bad choices didn't matter to them. He spent a lot of his spare time reading and writing inspirational literature. The Seeds Of Success, author unknown, is one of his favorite prayers. He prided himself on sharing what he had learned, and was leaning about life.

Financially Gordy wasn't poor. A relative had left Gordy a great deal of money, and a fairly large house, which he shared with his father and stepmother. Being an eighth grade teacher, and a part time weekend cab driver made it possible for him to share his knowledge with a variety of people.

It was past his bed time, but the actions of the day kept him awake. He decided to correct some school papers. An hour later he was finished and relax. All of his students received an A. With a smile on his face he prepared for bed.

Chapter Four

Sarah took a deep breath after she talked to the man she believed had saved her son's life. The love of her life was bitten by the bug. This bug had left a sting of emotional confusion. Her kid's heart had been blackened by it. He couldn't seem to get enough oxygen to his brain to think clearly. Deaf, dumb, and blind were his symptoms. The thought of these symptoms becoming fatal was breaking her heart. She felt Miss Mary's hand on her hand, shaking it lightly. "I'm sorry Miss Mary," Sarah said, as she reached for a napkin to wipe her eyes. Sarah finished her lukewarm coffee, and picked up the report to read it again.

As she was reading the report, Miss Mary whispered her name and told her two policemen were coming their way. One asked if she was Ms. Sarah Willaby with a son named Samuel Willaby. "Yes I am, she told them. They told her they were there to get a report from her son, and were told that she might be in the cafeteria. Sarah offered them seats at the table. They sat, and were very polite when they introduced themselves as Officer Green and Officer Smith. The officers shared their highest regard for Mr. Mann's quick thinking and patience, along with what they knew about the scene. "Thank you very much," Sarah made eye to eye contact with both of the officers. "Samuel is in the surgery room now. I don't know if he'll be up to making a statement when he comes out. But the doctor has suggested that he stay for a few days."

The two officers agreed to come back the next day. The two left after they shook Miss Mary's and Sarah's hands, and wished Samuel a speedy recovery. Sarah looked at Miss Mary. It was understood between the two that it was time to check on Samuel. Sarah picked up the report and placed it in her purse before the two got up, gathered their empty cups and left the cafeteria.

The ladies room was the first room the two went into. After they freshened up Sarah turned to Miss Mary. "Miss Mary thank you for being with me. You and I are working so hard to get Samuel back on the right track. I never thought he'll become so self-centered and without self control."

Miss Mary took both of Sarah's hands in hers and gave her a smile. She told Sarah to cheer up and to remember that trouble don't always last.

"But Miss Mary..."

Miss Mary led her to the mirror, and told her to whistle.

"Whistle?" Sarah tried but couldn't without laughing.

The two walked to the elevator arm in arm laughing. Sarah kept trying to stop laughing in the elevator, but Miss Mary had her going.

Sarah and Miss Mary saw Samuel's doctor coming down the hall when they got off the elevator. The doctor smiled and stood still when he saw them. The two saw him place his pen in his pocket, and after taking off hiss glasses place them there too. When they were face to face, the two noticed the doctor looking at the tears in their eyes which had came from laughing. He told them there was no need to be sad, and had them follow him. Samuel was asleep in the recovery room with the same bags and tubes running in his arm. The two were told by the doctor that Samuel would be monitor through the night. "I plan to spent the night," Sarah told the doctor.

The doctor looked her in the eye, and suggested that she go home and get a good night's sleep, because Samuel would be doing the same. Miss Mary agreed and helped to convince her. The two thanked the doctor, gave Samuel some light kisses on the cheek and forehead, and left the hospital.

"Drive carefully. I'll see you at home Miss Mary," Sarah said going to her car. Miss Mary asked if Sarah wanted to race.

"Oh Miss Mary!" Sarah laughed. "Oh, I almost forgot," Sarah said and reached in her purse. "Here, It's just a token." Miss Mary took the money and thanked Sarah. After she got in her car, she followed Miss Mary to their home. After both parked, they walked together to their homes. The two said goodnight at their doors.

Sarah was very tried when she ran her bubble bath water. The water felt good, but her mind was clouded with the thought of today. Something Miss Mary had said interrupted her thoughts. "Trouble don't always last, I pray it doesn't, she whispered." She leaned back and closed her eyes for a few minutes. After her bath she retired to the comforts of her bed.

CHAPTER FIVE

Samuel was a little scared when he woke up early in the hospital. He saw he was in a room with two beds. Someone was in the other bed. He relaxed a bit. "Mom?," he said quietly. "Mom," he called a little louder. Maybe she was awake all night looking at me, he thought. Samuel looked around. He wanted to get up, but the bags and tubes wouldn't let him. "Mom," he called much louder.

Seconds later a nurse came in laughing. She told him she saw him on the monitor and how cute he looked calling the patient Mom. Samuel was a little embarrassed but she made him laugh about it. "Can't I get up?" Samuel asked. He didn't know how difficult it was going to be, until he tried to move his cast thigh.

The nurse removed the tubes, and helped him to sit up. She told him she had crutches for him at the nurse's station. Twenty minutes later she had helped him to get up and was showing him how to use his crutches. She helped him to get to the bathroom, and to get back into the bed. Samuel noticed that his room mate was still sleeping in spite of the talking in the room. Samuel smelled the breakfast food and became hungry. "What time is breakfast?" he asked.

The nurse looked at her watch and told him in less than an hour. She started gathering all the equipment, and took it when she left the room. He leaned back and closed his eyes. He began to think about his father. His father's absence made him feel helpless. There was no blood strength he could turn to. Making bad choices seemed to give him strength and recognition. His love for his father needed to be embraced. Most of the time he felt sad, but his father kept telling him to be strong. "Listen to your mama boy," his father always said before walking away. Maybe I'll see my dad in jail. This thought made him smile.

Someone was calling his name. Samuel opened his eyes. It was his breakfast. His room mate was sitting up, and waiting for his. His room mate looked to be a hundred years old. He seemed to look at him, but Samuel focused his eyes back to his tray. The food was good, but it wasn't like his moms's. Samuel was drinking his milk when his mom walked in with a small suitcase in her hand. He very happy to see her, and even though she gave him a hug and kiss, he knew, that she knew what had happened.

"I brought your game boy, and some of your art supplies." Sarah walked over and turned on the T.V. "This phone is on too. How do you feel?"

"I feel much better. Can I go home today." Sarah walked to the closet with the suitcase in her hand, she opened it, and took out some clothes to place in the closet.

"Samuel you scarred me, but I thank God, and you should to, for being alive."

"Mom I can't remember what happened."

"Do you remember running away?"

"Yes, now I do! A man was chasing me."

"Why?" Sarah placed her hand on her son's shoulder.

"He must have thought I took something from the store."

"Did you?"

Before Samuel could answer, the two officers she met yesterday walked in.

"Good morning officers," Sarah greeted them. "My son said he can't remember too much."

Both of the officers greeted Samuel. One told him Samuel to listen carefully, and tell them if the report was true or not.

Samuel closed his eyes. Sarah shook his shoulders a little. "Please keep your eyes open."

The officers read the report and then asked Samuel if it was true.

"No," Samuel said. Samuel was asked if he took a Mr. Mann's wallet.

"No," Samuel said again.

The other officer asked him if he had seen the face of the man who chased him.

"I was too scared to look at his face," Samuel said nervously.

The officers informed Sarah and Samuel that Mr. Mann did not want to press charges because he found his wallet on the other side of the fence. Sarah looked at the officers for a few minutes. They were looking at Samuel who had closed his eyes. Finally Sarah spoke up. "I have spoken to Mr. Mann, and we will be meeting with him when Samuel comes home," Sarah said to the officers. She noticed Samuel was peeping at them..

Officer Smith asked about Samuel's father. Samuel opened his eyes. "He's incarcerated, " Sarah told them. The officers showed empathy.

Before leaving they wished Samuel get well soon, and told him to never take anything that didn't belong to him. They thanked the two and left. Sarah moved the tray table away from the bed. "You get some rest honey. I'll be over here in this big comfortable chair."

The nurse came in with some medication for Samuel, and his room mate. Sarah thanked her, and leaned back in the chair. She then asked Samuel if he needed anything.

"Yea mom can I have some donuts, candy, and chips?"

"How bout if I go to the store across the street and get you a bag of ginger snaps? You like them and they're good for you."

"Okay, and some milk to please," he said, before Sarah left the room.

While Sarah was at the store a nurse helped Samuel to get up, because it was time to make the beds. Samuel grabbed his game boy, but was unable to carry it while using his crutches. While Samuel was standing up the nurse put an extra hospital gown from the back on him. He was told to practice using his crutches. The nurse helped him twice from room to the front desk. Sarah was surprise to see Samuel using his crutches when she got off the elevator. Samuel looked up and saw her. "Mom stay there."

Sarah stopped, and leaned against a wall because she knew it was going to be a long wait. Her mind took her back twelve years ago, and she heard herself say again to her son. "Come on, come on you can make it."

Finally, Samuel made it to her smiling. Sarah opened the cookie bag and put one in his mouth. "I'm proud of you. Are you tired?" He nodded his head yes.

"These things can hold you up while you rest," Samuel said while chewing and demonstrating. The two took a very slow walk back to his room.

"I stopped at the cafeteria and got some cups and napkins. We'll get you cleaned up and changed before our snacks. Okay?"

Samuel sat back in the comfortable chair and watched his mother move around the room. She knows. "Why hasn't she yelled at me?" Samuel wondered. His mother's kindness sometimes made him felt bad for the wrong things he did. That man didn't have to save me, he thought. He knew he was taught in the gang not to show comparison for himself or anyone else. Also not to be afraid of dying. This thought lead to the next thought, I never want to die and never be able to do nothing! But I don't want to be weak in front of my boys either. If only I could talk to my father, maybe...

"Son, I'm going to help you into the bathroom. You can brush your teeth. I'll help you with the upper part of you. After you finish, I'll put you back in the bed and put an towel under your legs and feet so I can wash them."

"Mom, maybe I can just take a shower," Samuel said frowning at all the work of washing up.

" We'll have to ask your doctor that, but for the time being, this is the way it's got to be done. Then we can have a snack."

Samuel sighed, but took the crutches from his mother and the two went into the bathroom. After all was done, Samuel fell asleep before he had his snack. Sarah ate cookies and milk in the comfortable chair and she too fell asleep watching T.V.

CHAPTER SIX

Gordy looked at his clock. He had slept a little longer than usual. He took a shower and got dressed. As usual breakfast was already prepared, which he had with his newspaper. An hour later he was sitting in his cab. Sunday mornings were good. Some people were going to church, others needed a cab because of the Sunday bus schedule. Most of his riders were regulars, who found it easy to talk to him. Gordy had to learn to treat people the way he wanted to be treated the hard way. He took a vow with God not to take anyone for granted. Five, O'clock came quick. It was time for Gordy to pick up five of the boys on his basketball team. The rest of the team were brought to the church for practice or a game by their parents, who were mostly mothers and grandmothers. Each boy he picked up was greeted with a smile and a firm hand shake.

All team members, coachers, and referees had to be ready and on the court floor at 6:30. Every practice and game was taped to watch later. The boys were twelve and thirteen. At these ages, Gordy knew they needed meditation to unwind. His approach was to help the boys learn how to pray, and breathe correctly. So before each game or practice Gordy would blow his whistle. The team, coaches, and referees joined hands as they stood before the hops on the gym floor. The people on the benches also stood up.

Gordy had given everyone who were involved with the team eight sentences of a poem to learn and recite together. Before the sentences were said, they inhaled deeply and exhaled slowly four times. He felt proud of his team dressed in their black and gold short sets. He thought about himself at thirteen when he held hands with two of his team members, who stood on each side. He hoped that he too could make an impression like so many had done for him. The breathing was preformed, and everyone who knew the poem began to say it.

"God I thank you for this day. I know I have not accomplish as yet all that YOU expect of me. And it that is YOUR reason for bathing me in the fresh dew of another dawn I am most grateful. I am prepared, at last to make you proud of me.

I will forget yesterday with all it's trails and tribulations, aggravations, setbacks, anger, and frustrations. The past is already a dream from which I can neither retrieve a single word nor erase any foolish deeds. I will resolve, however, that if I have injured anyone through my thoughtlessness, I will not let this day's sun set before I make amends, and nothing I do will be of greater importance. I will not fret the future. My success and happiness does not depend on my straining to see what lurks dimly on the horizon but to do this day what lies clearly at hand. I will treasure this day, for it is all I have. I know it's rushing hours cannot be stored like precious grain for future use. Amen!

Everyone clapped. Those in the benches took their seats, and the whistle was blown. The game began. Gordy team played hard and the two teams were tied for a while, but the tie was broke by Gordy's team and they won. High fives, hugs, and joyful laugher was done by the team. Both teams grabbed water and chips before relaxing to view the video. This was always the most fun. The video captured the details of every play. Afterwards it was cleanup time before leaving the building.

"Win or lose, I'm proud of my team for"...

"STAYING OUT OF TROUBLE!" they all yelled. The boys called Gordy, Big Guy, even though he didn't have a large body frame or tall.

"Do your best," Gordy hollered after each boy got out of his cab. It was still a beautiful day, when he dropped the last boy off. With a smile on his face, Gordy turned up the jazz that was playing on the radio and headed home.

CHAPTER SEVEN

Samuel was wakened up for lunch. His mother was still in the comfortable chair reading a magazine. "Mom are you going to have lunch?" Samuel asked, looking for the salt and pepper.

"Samuel, say thank you to the nurse first," his mom told him with raised eyebrows.

"Thank you," Samuel said putting salt and pepper on his carrots and mashed potatoes. Samuel looked across the room. The old man's hand looked old and ashy, and a lot of veins ran through them. He looked directly in Samuel's eyes.

Samuel looked away, and picked up some food. Moments later, a woman about his mother's age and a girl about his age came into the room. When they saw the old man their faces lit up. Both gave him a kiss and hug. The lady called him daddy, when she asked how did he feel. Samuel was surprised when he heard the man speak. His voice sounded like an younger man. The girl called him granddaddy when she told him she loved and missed him. Both pulled up chairs.

How can someone love someone that old? Samuel asked himself, while eating his food. Oh man! My mother, and my dad are going to be that old. He looked at his mother, who was still looking through the magazine. Suddenly he felt sorrow for them. Then he felt glad, because their getting old was a long way away.

His mother smiled and greeted the three people. She then wished them well, before she got up and walked over to Samuel. She helped him with his tray and wiped his mouth again. Samuel's eyes went over to the girl in the room. He was glad she was busy with her grandfather and hadn't saw his mother wipe his face.

His mother kept trying to make eye to eye contact with him. He pretended not to notice by picking up his game boy. Minutes later his mother left the room, and came back with a wheelchair.

His mother had a big smile on her face, when she told him she had seen a recreation room down the hall. She suggested the two of them could go there and check it out. Samuel wanted to kept that smile on his mother's face, and agreed to go. His mother made him comfortable in the wheelchair, with a pillow under his thigh. She grabbed her purse, the cookies and milk. He held the items on his lap as his mother pushed the wheelchair to the recreation room. Two people were on the far side of the room when they entered. His mother said, "Hi" quietly. After looking around the two decided to do a five hundred piece puzzle. He recalled what she had taught him. His mother took the items before she pushed him close to the table. Samuel reached for the box on the table and opened it. He emptied the pieces out in front of himself and his mother, who had taken a chair across from him. The bottom and top of the box was placed in front of the pieces. The task began as each piece was examined by both. If a piece was for the border of the puzzle, it was put into one box. The middle pieces of the puzzle was put into the other box. Samuel enjoyed the way his mother bragged about finding pieces.

"See this piece?" Sarah asked her son and held the piece as close as she could to Samuel's face. "I know where this piece goes," she said, and placed the piece. The two made one another laugh as the puzzle came together.

"Now that I have your attention Samuel Willaby, I want you to tell me the truth." His mother's eyes told him, she meant business!

"I know where this piece goes," he said. He was given THE NOW-look.

"Okay...it was three of us in the store. Some of my friends you haven't met yet. One of my friends snatched the man's wallet. I forgot his name. I decided to run to throw the man off. His mother's face changed as if he had just hit her. She leaned over the table and became inches from his face.

"Samuel he found his wallet near the fence."

"I think my boy ran down that street and hide it there."

"Tell me what the man looked like."

"I don't know! Everything happened so fast. I was too scared to look at him."

"No, no young man I smell a rat. But you know I will find out." Sarah placed a few pieces of the puzzle in place before she spoke again.

"It's always best to tell the truth up front and get it over with. That way you'll show you're sorry for what you did. Good people sometimes make terrible mistakes, but they will tell the truth. Samuel please don't be a bad person who steals and lies."

"Okay, don't believe me than. Sarah looked at him, he avoided her eyes.

"Are you lying?" Sarah held her breath.

"No, he said, looking for another piece. Sarah's heart was broken. She poured two cups of milk and gave her son one. Samuel reached for the cookies. He opened them and held them toward his mother. She shook her head no. He took out a hand full and placed them on the table, before closing the bag. The puzzle and milk were finished before all his cookies were.

"There's nothing in this world that would make me stop loving you. Do you know that?" Sarah said, while she prepared for them to leave this room.

"Yea," was all Samuel said while his mother pushed him back to the room.

CHAPTER EIGHT

The old man's family was still in the room. They were watching T.V., and laughing together. The old man seem to look younger to Samuel. Samuel was glad to get back on the bed. He closed his eyes. He was awaken by the doctor. The doctor told them that Samuel couldn't go back to school for a week, and that it would be two weeks before the cast would be removed. Samuel's mind began to rush with thoughts of girls feeling sorry for him. A nurse shook him to give him medication. Before drifting back to sleep, he heard the old man's family tell him to have an good night, and tomorrow he'd be in his own bed.

Sarah was still in the comfortable chair when she told Samuel's room mate's family goodnight. She was happy to see how much they cared for him. God is good, she thought. She became thirsty and wanted something cold to drink. She stood up, and looked at Samuel sleeping. She looked at her watch. It would be another two hours before Samuel would have dinner. He probably will sleep until then she thought, as she waited for the elevator. Sarah saw Samuel's roommate going down the hall just before she stepped in the elevator.

She smelled the aroma of the food coming from the elevator when the elevator door opened on the first floor. She decided to have an salad with her ice tea. She had just sat down with food and drink, when her cell phone rang. "Hello."

"Hello, is this Ms. Willaby?" Gordy asked. Sarah known Mr. Mann's voice.

"Yes it is Mr. Mann, but I'm in the hospital's cafeteria. Can I call you back in about fifteen minutes?"

"Sure that'll be fine," Gordy told her. She closed her phone and put it back in her purse. After she finished eating she took the elevator, and went to the recreation room. No one was in the room, so she felt at ease to talk on the phone. She pressed dial back on her phone. Seconds later Gordy answered.

"Hello Ms. Willaby, how is your son during?"

"He's doing better, thank you. He'll be going home tomorrow, but he has to wear a thigh cast for two weeks. I hope and pray that every step he takes will remind him to never take what's not his."

"Well, I'm glad he's doing better, and I hope also, that this experience will make him a better person."

"Mr. Mann, I'm glad you called. I would like to invite you to lunch on Sunday, at 3:00.

"Ms. Willaby, I'll love to come to lunch Sunday, but..."

"I think I know how you feel, but my son needs to admit he's done wrong, then apologize to you, and both of us can think you in person."

"Okay Ms. Willaby, I'll come Sunday. I have your address on the police report. Please tell your son I asked about him."

"Thank you Mr. Mann, I'll tell him." I live in a black and white building in apartment 7c. Have a good evening. I hope to see you soon."

"You will, and you have a good evening too." Sarah put her phone back in her purse and left the room. She walked down the hall to Samuel's room. When she got to the door she was surprise to see the nurse and Samuel's room mate standing around her son's bed. As she approached she heard her son say, he didn't see a watch.

"What's going on?" She asked them. The nurse spoke up, and told her, Mr. Jake said, he placed his watch on his stand before he went into the bathroom. Sarah looked at her watch, before she looked at her son. She had been gone a little over an hour.

"Did you get up while I was gone?" ,she asked her son.

"I got up to use the bathroom," he answer.

"Where was Mr. Jake?" Sarah asked.

"He was in the bathroom, I stood by the window and waited for him to come out."

Everyone was silent for a few minutes. The nurse announced that she had to get back to the station. She told everyone she would keep an eye out for the watch, she walked toward the door. Mr. Jake thanked her, and walked back to his bed. Sarah's heart was beating fast at Samuel's bedside.

"Son, do you still believe in God?" She asked while placing a pillow under his thigh. Samuel looked past her when he answered, "I guess so." Sarah got a brush, and begun brushing his hair. While she was brushing his hair, his dinner was brought in.

"Um that looks good," Sarah said, and thanked the nurse. Samuel put seasonings on his food and avoided her eyes.

"You enjoy your food, and I'll sit over here and watch T.V.." She walked over to the big chair. This was starting to become a nightmare she thought as she sat down. She glanced over at Mr. Jake, he saw her worried glance and nodded with an understanding smile to her.

Fifteen minutes later Samuel was finished with his dinner. Sarah helped him remove his tray table. She then helped him to get up and walked with him into the bathroom, where he was handed his toothbrush. "You're getting better with your crutches," she told her son, when he made it made it back from the bathroom. She helped him to get into the bed. "I put your game boy on the tray table. Honey, I'm going home now, but there's something I want you to so for me.

Samuel leaned back to listen to her. "The nurse is going to give you your medication, which you know will make you sleepy. If you need to go to the bathroom again, or need something to drink, press this button please Sam." Sarah placed the buttoncord close to Samuel. He agreed to use it. "I love you. If you took the watch, please give it to me now, and I will give it back to him. You will feel and do better," Sarah pleaded with all of her heart.

"I don't need his watch," he said and reached for his game boy box.

"Samuel I have an uneasy feeling. I'll be here early in the morning to take you home. Think about what I've said." She leaned to give him a kiss on the forehead.

She stood a few moments looking at her son with his eyes closed. Sarah told Mr. Jake to have a good night, before walking out of the room.

Sarah felt her eyebrows come together on her way out of the hospital. Did Samuel take Mr. Jack's watch? She knew he had snatched or played a big role in Mr. Mann's wallet. A thirteen year old liar and thief. Why? Samuel had chosen the hard road, she sighed and felt the tightness in her chest. Thank God for the cool air. It helped her to breathe a lot better on her way to the car. Once on the road, she tried to clear her head by remembering what Miss Mary told her,"Trouble don't last always." She was really tired when she got home, straight to the shower she went. After her shower she prepared Samuel's and her clothes for the next day.

Before going to bed, she found the watch her father had left her. She was saving it for Samuel, but...she said a prayer and went to bed.

Chapter Nine

Samuel took the medication and water from the nurse. He knew he should say thank you, but that was not him anymore. He wanted to be the bad boy. Samuel took out four cookies, and ate them with the milk from dinner. He noticed the old man looking at him, so he fixed his eyes on the T.V.. His mind started to wander. Last year he was called soft because he showed feelings of remorse. He has to mastered not caring about his mother's tears. He wanted to wear what he wanted, and do what he wanted to do. Being rebellious got him with other rebellious boys. He could smile now, but it was his jeans without a belt that had prevented him from climbing that fence faster that day. It was hard to play or practice any kind of sports with his new style. But he didn't care. Being cool and gangster like, seem to get the girls. He thought about the man who saved his life.

He hoped he'd never have to see the man who held his leg. Throwing his wallet away was an good idea. He got it back, and that should be all to it. He tried to picture the man's face but couldn't. Anyway, I got a watch to sell, and show my boys I'm good, he told himself. Being a gangster meant being a survivor. His thigh cast proved that he was.

Samuel started humming a song in his head. Do or die, yea, do or die. Last year his dreams to become a C.S.I. Investigator, or a professional ball player were replaced by being a gangster rapper. His thoughts of being a gangster rapper made him feel grown-up. All the words the rappers were singing became his words. Samuel decided to play his game boy. He took the rubber band from around the box he kept it in. Samuel had placed something else in the box. He took out what he needed to play with, and made sure the item on the bottom was covered up with game boy dices as he placed the box on the tray. It was less than an hour, when Samuel felt his eyes getting heavy. The old man's light was out when Samuel put his game away. He leaned back and closed his eyes. He wondered if his father had heard or thought about him. He didn't write too often. But he understood because he had other children by other women. He imagined his father telling everyone what a tough and bad little guy his son was. He had heard how his father dropped out of school, and been in and out of jail at an early age. Samuel yawned. Minutes later the medication took over.

Chapter Ten

"Wake up sleepy head," Sarah said, when she gently shook her son's shoulder.

"Hun...mom? What time is it?' Samuel asked, trying to focus his eyes.

"It's Seven-thirty. I told you I would come early." Sarah said, taking clothes from the suitcase she had brought in.

Samuel stretched. "I was thinking about Dad last night mom."

"Do you want to write him a letter?"

"Yes I want to tell him about my sticks." Samuel pointed to his crutches.

Sarah smiled. "Mr. Jake must be in the shower down the hall. His bed was empty when I came in."

"Maybe he couldn't sleep mom. Can I take a shower?"

"Let me go to the front desk and ask them."

"Mom, put the suitcase on the tray table, so I can put my books that I haven't read, and my game in it."

Sarah got the suitcase and placed it on the tray table. "Since you're in the mood for packing, pack these things too please." Sarah went to the closet, and took out Samuel's few clothes. All of the bloody clothes she had taken and thrown away. She picked up his bedroom shoes and placed them on his feet.

"These are your clothes for today." Sarah placed the clothes at the foot of the bed, and left the room.

Samuel put his game boy in first, then his books. He picked up clothes his mom took from the closet. He folded them, and placed them in the suitcase. Samuel closed the suitcase with the zipper.

"Good news Sam, the nurse is going to bring in a special plastic bag for your cast. She's going to show you how to use it when you take a shower today."

"Can I take it before I leave the hospital mom?"

"No, wait until you go home. The doctor has to examine you before you can be released to go home. Sarah removed the pillow from under Samuel's thigh. She put one hand on his shoulder.

"Come on it's time to get up and get ready for breakfast. "Here", she said, and handed Samuel his crutches. Samuel eased to the end of the bed and placed both feet on the floor. He took the crutches from his mom, stood up and headed for the bathroom. Sarah took the clothes he needed to put on, and followed behind him. She placed his socks in his sneakers before she placed them on the floor. While Samuel was at the sink, she placed his clothes on a hook behind the door. Then she left the bathroom and closed the door.

She greeted Mr. Jake, who was sitting on his bed fully dressed. His suitcase was shut, and on the bed. "Have you found your watch Mr. Jake?"

He told her he hadn't.

"Well I have something for you." Sarah got her purse and opened it. She reached in and pulled out a tissue wrapped watch.

"Here Mr. Jake, this is for you." Mr. Jake took it, and opened the tissue. His face lit up, then he looked closer. He told her it was not his watch.

"I know, but I want you to have his one. Please take it. It's my father's and it would mean so much to me if you took it."

Mr. Jake kept shaking his head, and told Sarah it was much too fancy. Finally she convinced him. The two hugged to say thanks and good-by. She walked over to the bed to finish packing. She noticed that Samuel had left one of his game boy discs out. She unzipped the suitcase and took out the game box. Taking off the rubber band, she opened the box to put the disc in. She was holding the box over the bed when it fell out of her hands. Tears and dismay came to Sarah's eyes.

She began to move fast. She picked up the watch, and put it in her pocket. She placed everything back in the box, which she put back in the suitcase, and zipped the suitcase. She then went over to Mr. Jake and exchanged watches. Finally she moved the suitcase to the big chair.

Samuel opened the door and called. "Mom, will you come here, and help me with my socks and sneakers?"

"Okay, I'll be there in a second." Sarah told him as she cleared off the stand. She glanced at Mr. Jake, and went into the bathroom.

"You look nice. I brought a pair of your large shorts to make it easy for you and the doctor." She bent down and took the socks out of the sneakers.

"Wow, your toenails are starting to look like a werewolves. Samuel laughed. I'm going to cut them when we get home." While Sarah was tying Samuel's sneakers, they heard the breakfast trays come in.

"Just in time," Samuel said gladly. Sarah stood up, and left the bathroom. Samuel stood up and grabbed his crutches. When he got one under each arm he came out of the bathroom. He looked at Mr. Jake with his tray, but didn't speak to him. He kept his eyes on his breakfast tray all the way to his bed. Sarah was standing by his bed, and assisted him with getting on it. She moved the tray closer to him, and walked into the bathroom. In the bathroom she picked up towels, his P.J.s and bedroom shoes. She gathered his toiletries which needed to be packed. She walked over to the suitcase unzipped it and put the items in. Before zipping it back, she looked at Samuel.

"Do you want me to take out your game boy box?"

"No mom. When it the doctor coming?" he asked her with a cup in his hand.

Sarah searched her son's face, before turning her attention back to zipping up the suitcase. "I hope it won't be much longer. It's still early...how bout if I go and get the wheelchair, and we go to the recreation room?" She looked at her son and waited for an answer.

"Okay mom, but I get to pick the puzzle." Samuel watched his mom leave out of the room. He was full, and wanted to go back to sleep. He pushed the tray table away, and leaned back. Just as he closed his eyes, he heard voices. It was the old man's family. Samuel kept his eyes closed and listened. There were three of them this time. The same two and a boy. His daughter asked him if he was packed, because the doctor had already signed his release papers. All of them sounded happy that he was coming home. When the nurse brought in the wheelchair, the boy and girl wanted to push it. Samuel heard the boy call him granddaddy, when he said he loved him. His daughter carried the suitcase, and within minutes the voices trailed the hallway.

Samuel opened his eyes. He wondered if those kids had a father in their life. He wondered if he had a grandfather in his life would they have been close. He knew what had happened to his mother's parents, but his dad never talked about his dad. I'll ask him in my letter, he told himself.

Samuel decided to get up, and go find his mother. He took his time and was almost at the door, when his mother came through it with a wheelchair. Sarah took the crutches and Samuel put each hand on the arms of the wheelchair. He sat down and his mother bent to pull out the feet support.

Sarah turned the wheelchair around, and the two faced the doctor. The doctor had on his glasses , and a board with papers on it. He asked Sarah to take Samuel back to the bed. She helped her son to sit on the bed. The doctor examined Samuel, and asked him questions about how he felt. "I feel fine. I'm ready to go home," he told him. The doctor told them, he would removed the cast in a week, and gave them the information. He also gave them prescriptions for antibiotics and pain. Sarah thanked the doctor. He then told them to wait for the nurse.

Sarah had almost forgot about the nurse bringing the plastic bag for Samuel's shower.

"Can I get back up?" Samuel asked the doctor. The doctor told him yes.

Sarah helped him to get back into the wheelchair. She gather the crutches and the suitcase to put by the door.

After the nurse gave them the demonstration of how to put the plastic bag on, and take it off, Samuel said, "Oh that is easy. I can't wait to take a shower." The nurse laughed and told them she had to walk them to their car. Sarah placed the suitcase on Samuel's lap. The nurse pushed the wheelchair, and Sarah carried the crutches. Samuel waved goodby to the staff and Sarah thanked them all.

It was a beautiful day outside, when Sarah went to get the car, while the nurse and Samuel waited by the entrance. Minutes later, Samuel was helped in the car and both waved goodby to the nurse, before heading home.

CHAPTER ELEVEN

Gordy picked up his keys and lunch from the kitchen counter. Have a good day was always wrote on the front of his lunch bag. His good day seem to start when he read it. With brief case in his hand he yelled, "Have a good day." Closing the door he spotted the people he had yelled to in the garden. "Good morning you two," Gordy said with a smile and a little laugh, because he had already bid them a good day. He preceded to his car.

As usual he was early. He enjoyed going to the teacher's lounge to have his pastry from his lunch bag and coffee, along with conversations with several staff members. Gordy's unique way of teaching was getting results. He made sure to start his class with meditation and a poem. He was clever enough to give the other half of the poem, The Seeds Of Success, to his class. Since prayer was banned, he didn't want any negative feed back. The principal and most teachers and parents were impressed with Gordy's students. The allegiance will always be done...but afterwards Gordy showed his class how to relax while breathing, and to make a commitment to them self, by using the poem.

Gordy was one of the teachers who went outside to greet and inspect the conduct and dress code of the children before they enter the school building. This took a little extra time, but job readiness was the focus of the school. The children who were being respectful and dressed correct, went through the front door to the cafeteria for breakfast. The others went through the side door, and were sent to the gym. In the gym, they wrote their names on a sheet of paper, and their excuses for breaking the rules. A teacher in the gym would read and correct their papers. Any word they got wrong had to be written twenty times. After the corrections some went to the guidance office, the rest, one at a time stood in front of a mirror. They were asked to choose from several boxes of articles of clothing. Some boxes contained under wares, socks, belts, shirts or pants. Any articles that would help them to complete the dress code were to be chosen. Because their names were put on the black broads , they were allowed to leave their classes ten minutes earlier to return the articles. Quite a few children Gordy met found it hard to share their life in a good way with others. He enjoyed working with, and teaching children the true meaning of being born. His father still represented a good role model in his life. He always encouraged him to be a role model for children with or without fathers.

"Good morning, my people," Gordy said to his class when he enter the room with his brief case in his hand. Some stood and clapped their hands, because they had heard about the winning game. Others said good morning, but seconds later they all were seated to acknowledged his presence. Ten O'clock, the principal's voice is heard. "Will everyone please stand." He lead everyone in the pledge of allegiance. Afterward, he announced all the children's birthdays for that day, before putting the microphone down, he told the children to do the best in everything they do.

Gordy's class knew to remain standing. Gordy stood in front of the class, and as usual spoke softly. "Please close your eyes and relax. This is a new day. Somebody loves you. Don't make the same mistakes. Take a deep breath." Gordy waited a few seconds. "Blow it out. Keep your eyes closed and repeat after me." Gordy watched the children while they repeated what he said. "I will waste not even a precious second today in anger or hate or jealousy or selfishness. I will face the world with goals set for this day, but they will be attainable ones, not the vague, impossible variety, declared by those who make a career of failure. I realize that you always try me with a little first, to see what I would do with a lot.

"I will never hide my talents. If I am silent, I am forgotten, if I do not advance,

I will fall back. If I walk away from any challenge today, my self-esteem will be forever scarred, and if I cease to grow, even a little, I will become smaller. I reject the stationary position because it is always the beginning of the end."

Gordy clapped his hands, and the children opened their eyes and sat down.

He went to his desk, picked up his brief case and took out some papers. He called each child up and gave them their test paper. Their eyes lit up when they saw their grades. Their smiles and Hi-fives touched his heart and made his eyes shine like diamonds. "I hope you all like pizza and chicken wings."

Gordy stopped for a few minutes. A pin dropped could have been heard. His class waited for him to finished. "Because that's what we are going to have for lunch." More hi-fives were done. Gordy turned and walked to the black board and picked up the chalk.

He started writing on the broad, and behind him was the noise of the children preparing to take notes. All of them turned on their tape recorders. Recording and taking notes, which Gordy supervised, helped his class to focus. The children listened to the recordings with headphones during study time each day. Each one's tape recorder stayed in school under lock and key. On the black broad Gordy wrote, Good Morning, the number of the lesson, and in bigger letters PAY ATTENTION. He then began showing his class math problems and asking questions. Everyone was addressed by their last names, with Mister or Miss in front. When he called their names they were required to stand. Later that morning Gordy took the time to order pizza.

Because of his father's sayings, "Practice makes perfect," he gave tests and homework everyday. Gordy soon found out that it was more than an saying, it was a fact. He made an habit of talking about his two favorite people, his father, and his step mother, who lived with him. The days for him seem to fly by, and before he knew it, he heard people saying, TGIF, thank God it's Friday. On Fridays, Gordy collected the notebooks. Any missing notes or examples needed he inserted with a word of encouragement, before he handed them back on Mondays. "Have a good weekend," Gordy told his class. When all the children had left his class room, he packed his brief case with notebooks and papers. As usual he went home to prepare for his football practice.

Gordy turned his key and opened the door to the most delicious aroma. Fresh cinnamon rolls had been baked and placed on the table. After placing his brief case on the counter, he washed his hands, poured a glass of milk, and grabbed a cinnamon roll. After taking a bite, he placed it on a napkin. He sat down at the kitchen table and picked up the remote and turned to sports channel. Seconds later he was turning his head from side to side. God is good, and so is this roll, with a smile he took another one. When he had finished his milk he was full. He relaxed a little at the table while he watched a basketball game. He stood up and stretched , before he picked up the empty milk glass and put it in the dish washer.

Gordy went to his room and changed quickly into a sleeveless shirt, shorts, sneakers and a headband. Before he got to the sliding doors, he saw his dad in the dinning room relaxing. The two smiled at one another. "Want to play a few games?," Gordy asked him.

His dad got up and told Gordy to give him a few minutes to change. Gordy went through the doors and picked up a basketball from the shack. The echo sound of Gordy bounding the ball on the pavement could be heard through the house. He had made a few hoops shots before he dad came out.

"Are you ready for a beat down?" Gordy asked him. His dad smiled and knocked the ball out of Gordy's hands. The two played until it was time for Gordy to shower and get dressed.

"I'll see you later dad," Gordy said and went through the silding doors.

Gordy had given his dad, who acted like the butler, a list and money to go to the warehouse for groceries. Boxes of individual snack bags, and water for the team were on the list. Before leaving the house, Gordy got a box of snacks and water for his team. His step mother, who acted like the maid, was in the kitchen preparing dinner. "Mom, those cinnamon rolls brought tears of joy to my eyes and mouth." His step mother laughed and fanned him on.

I'll see you two later," he said at the door. After putting the water and snacks in the trunk of the car, Gordy got in and proceeded to pick up the boys.

All the boys were ready and glad to see him. Once in the parking lot of the church, the boys got out and helped to carry items from the trunk into the building. There was much laugher during the viewing of the last game video. After the tape the breathing techniques were done, and the SEEDS OF SUCCESS, was said before their practice. The video camera was in place, and the parents and friends and the people in the stands cheered them on. The practice went by fast, and now it was time to clean up the water bottles and empty snack bags. When this was done, Gordy called his team together, and with a bottle of water in his hand he took the center ring. His team was sweaty, but they all stood around him with smiles. "Young men, all of you are getting better, and I appreciate that. Until I see you guys Sunday, keep a good heart and treat people...before Gordy could finish the sentence, the whole team shouted. "THE WAY YOU WANT TO BE TREATED."

Gordy laughed. "There is a God, see you all Sunday." An hour later, Gordy was back home at the dinner table with his favorite two people.

CHAPTER TWELVE

Sarah parked her car as close to her apartment as she could in the tenant's area. "Stay put Samuel until I come around to open the door and help you."

Samuel looked around the building, searching for one of his boys. Sarah opened the back door first and took out the crutches. Samuel opened the car door and moved one leg out. Sarah helped him to move closer to the door. Finally he stood up, and took the crushes from his mother. Sarah waited until both crutches were in place. "You start walking to the house while I get the suitcase and lock the doors. Sarah stood and watched her son moving with the crutches. He was doing well, but he seemed to be looking for someone. With the suitcase in her hand she caught up with him. After she unlocked the house doors she placed the suitcase inside. "Here, let me help you."

Samuel looked at his mom. She's so soft, she's too soft. She knows what I did to get my thigh cut. Samuel thought this, but said,

"Let me do this mom."

Sarah looked in her son's eyes. My baby is in there somewhere. Who or what is my son trying to be.? Sarah shook these thoughts and said,

"Okay," as she walked in front of him. The two heard footsteps coming down the starts. Miss Mary called her honey, as she came in and gave her a hug. She invited Sarah to lunch. "Miss Mary, I'll be up for lunch, but first I have to find my ready to use camera." Sarah moved fast as she looked here and there. "Oh here it is!" She began to tell Samuel to look up and smile while she took serval pictures of him with crutches.

"Hi Miss Mary," Samuel finally said.

Miss Mary gave him a hug and told him she was glad to see him. She squeezed his shoulders and told him she thanked God for him being alive. Samuel didn't say anything as he waited until Miss Mary let him go. He walked out of the kitchen to his room. "Mom can you bring my suitcase in my room please?" Samuel had sat on the bed, the suitcase was brought in. Sarah placed it on the bed.

"Thank you, is Miss Mary still here?"

"Yes, but I'll be back in a few." Sarah left the room.

Samuel pulled the suitcase closer and unzipped it. He removed his game boy box. He looked toward the door before he took off the rubber band from the game boy box. "OH man!" His mind was thinking that the old man must have gotten up through the night or maybe early in the morning and took the watch back. He looked through everything that was in the suitcase again. He shook his head. His mom appeared at the door.

"I"ve got the bathroom set up for your shower." She walked closer to the bed and picked up the empty suitcase. Samuel prepared to stand up, while his mother separated the clothes and items. "Here's the shower bag. There's a chair in the tub. Take your time and call me when you're in the chair.

"Okay," Samuel said, on his way out of the room. Got you! Sarah thought while watching her son leave the room. God please help my son, she prayed while clearing off the bed.

"Mom I need you!"

"Okay, I'll be right there." Sarah remembered she needed to cut her son's toenails, so she got the toenails clippers to take with her. Samuel had wrapped a towel around him, and was sitting sideways on the chair in the bathtub with his feet hanging with socks and sneakers still on. She sat on the floor in front of her son's feet. After taking off his sneakers and socks, she clipped his toe nails. Neither one of them spoke. When she was finished she asked, "Where is that plastic bag you need for the shower?"

"On the sink." After Sarah retrieved it the two placed it on. Sarah picked up the shampoo and turned on the water. After she lathered Samuel's head, she reached for the shower head and began to rise it.

"Samuel why did you take Mr. Jake's watch?"

Samuel opened his eyes at the wrong time. "My eyes! My eyes!"

Sarah helped her son to get the soap out of his eyes.

"I don't have his watch!" Samuel said, while still wiping his eyes with the wash cloth.

"Did you take his watch?" Sarah asked while she washed his back.

"Hold your legs straight so I can wash your feet." Sarah began to wash her son's feet.

"Why are you stealing and lying?"

Samuel didn't answer.

"I love you, but you don't love me. Your hurting my heart. Samuel remained silent pouting. She could tell he was trying not to care.

"If you want to talk to me about anything, I'll listen." Sarah stood up. "Make sure you wash your ears so you can hear me. Scrub your neck, and the rest of your body good. Everything you need to put on is on the door." Sarah left the bathroom. "Call me if you need me," she said, before she closed the bathroom door.

Samuel wanted to tell his mom thank you, for making his head, back, and feet feel good. But now there was him stealing the watch. How can I tell her I stole the watch? She already knows it was me who took that man's wallet. She acts like she can't believe I can do or say these things. She doesn't understand, I'm trying to get an gangster reputation. I don't want to be soft. I'm going to write about my life. Yea. One of these days. Besides mom is too soft about this love thing. Some of my friend's mothers don't care what they do. They are cool. They party a lot and are lazy about life. Why can't my mother be more like them? Besides I know my mother would never give up on me. She cries because she loves me, but I got to be tough like my dad. Samuel smelled something good in the kitchen and decided to hurry up.

Sarah had finished cooking for lunch and dinner, when Samuel came out of the bathroom.

"Come and have your lunch. I made pork shops, mashed potatoes, and peas and carrots. This is going to be for dinner too. I took the cord to your T.V.. You are grounded for stealing and lying." Samuel sat down and began to eat. He was almost finished when his mom came back into the kitchen. She didn't smile.

"It's time for your medication.' Samuel opened his mouth and she placed the pills in. He picked up his milk and washed them down. Sarah left the kitchen again. Samuel waited at the table with a half a glass of milk. His mom came back into the kitchen. "Finish your milk and go to your room." Samuel looked at his mom. He got up and made it to his room. He had wanted some dessert. He got into bed with his game boy. His mother came into his room with the phone.

"If you need me call me upstairs." Sarah left.

She thinks she can make me weak. Samuel thought and began to pout. He felt it ,but had to be strong. The kissing and hugs had to stop sooner or later. He got up and went into the kitchen. He got some ice cream and cookies, which he took back to his room to eat. This made him feel better. When he finished he leaned over on his bed and pushed the bowl under his bed. Samuel felt himself getting sleepy, but he wanted to write his father. Picking up a pen and paper from his bed stand he began to write. When he finished he signed it, your dog, holler back. Putting the pen down he folded the paper, and placed it on the bed stand. Samuel got comfortable in the bed and before long he went to sleep.

CHAPTER THIRTEEN

Miss Mary had prepared a nice chef's salad for their lunch. The two ate and talked about news, church, and Samuel. After Sarah told Miss Mary about the watch, the two agreed Samuel needed a mentor or counseling, and maybe both. "I'll start looking Monday," Sarah said as she sipped her orange juice. "Tomorrow is Saturday. Maybe I should call off...Miss Mary stopped her and told her she'd look after Samuel tomorrow. "Oh! Miss Mary, I forgot to tell you about the guy who saved Samuel's life, Mr. Mann is coming to dinner Sunday.

Miss Mary clapped her hands like it was music to her ears, and asked if Samuel knew. "No, not yet, but I think I'll tell him tomorrow when I come home.," Sarah smiled with Miss Mary. Miss Mary asked if she could meet him. "Sure you can at dinner, please come. It's at 3:00." Minutes later Sarah prepared to leave. Miss Mary stood up and gave her a hug. "I'll see you tomorrow Miss Mary, but I'll call you later to say good night. Thank you for the lunch and a reason to smile."

Sarah opened her door and after locking it, went straight to Samuel's room. Samuel was asleep. She watched him for a few minutes. I'll be glad Lord, when he stops playing make believe in a real world. As she prayed, she noticed a piece of paper lying on the floor close to the night stand. She picked it up, and went into the living room. She placed the folded paper on the coffee table and lay down on the couch. She looked at the paper on the coffee table, and decided to read it. It read; Dear home boy how you be. I chilling. My leg almost got cut off. But It didn't so I will walk with sticks. I had something for you like a watch but I will get you another one. I am like scare face. You can call me scar thigh. Your dog holler back.

Sarah couldn't believe it. First, he had stole a watch for his father. Secondly he wrote as if he wasn't even from this world. She decided to put the letter on his stand and ask him about it later. Samuel was still asleep when she went back into his room and placed the letter on the bed stand. After closing the door Sarah went back into the living room and lay on the couch. She knew her son could read, because she had helped him to learn everyday since he was born. She turned on some music to relax herself. But her mind kept coming back to Samuel's behavior. She was taught that everything you do in the dark will come to the light, sooner or later. Samuel needed to learn and remember this. Maybe she shouldn't tell Samuel the name of their Sunday guest or who he really was.

She began to smile when other thoughts came to mind. For dinner we'll have Cornish hens, yams, potato salad , and mushrooms and peas. Her smile got broader, when she visualized what might happen on Sunday. The music was sounding good,

she was humming when she got up, got her purse and opened it. After taking out her father's watch, she went and placed it on the kitchen table. She went back on the couch and took a nap.

She had sleep for a few hours. Her first thought was Samuel. She felt rested when she got up from the couch. Samuel's door was still closed. She opened the door. Samuel was coming toward the door.

"Hi mom," he said quietly. "I've got to go to the bathroom."

"Come into the kitchen when you're finished please," Sarah said as she turned to go there. Minutes later Samuel appeared in the kitchen. "Do you want to get your letter ready for the mail?" Sarah watched her son's reactions.

"Oh yea, I almost forgot." Samuel continued to his room. Sarah followed.

"Have you finished the letter?"

" Yea. Oh here it is."

"Samuel please bring another piece of paper." She heard her son say something.

"Tell me at the kitchen table."

Sarah was seated with the letter opened, and the watch on top of it. Samuel came into the kitchen, and placed the pen and paper down on the table. He took a seat across from his mother. His eyes fell on the watch.

"Whose watch is that?"

Sarah gave him the watch. She watched him look at it and feel the unusual designs on it.

"This watch was my father's. I was saving it for your high school graduation. I hope that you'll be more mature then. I have to know that you'll pass it to your children, along with the knowledge of what it takes to a for real person. Your having troubles now, but there are ways you can fix or overcome your short comings. If you want to get better, there are people to help you. My father earned this watch. You will have to earn it too. Having a good heart will stop you from doing a lot of wrong deeds. Do you want this watch?"

"This is a nice watch, it looks like it costed a lot of money." Samuel said, being enthrall by the watch.

"You can't answer my question now, but I hope and pray that you will in the near future."

Sarah took the watch from her son.

"I read your letter to your father. And if you want your father to feel bad about you, you can sent this one. You have got to feel sorry about doing wrong, before you can do right. Maybe you can let your father feel that your going to be a better person. That your not trying to go to jail or die an early death. Sarah got up from the table with the watch.

Samuel picked up his letter and read it again. It sounded good to him.

"Walk with sticks," he said in a whisper, made him smile. The truth was, he didn't feel bad about the things he did. He was glad he didn't die, but do or die was what he was learning. All his boys said the same thing. "I don't care." He wanted to be like them.

"Do you want me to help you rewrite your letter to your father?. He mother asked after she came back into the kitchen and sat down next to him.

"No that's all right. I'll sent him this one." Sarah wanted to scream, YOU REALLY DON'T GET IT, but her heart for her confused son wouldn't let her say a word. Her son wouldn't look at her. But she knew he felt her pain. She gave him the envelope with his father's address on it, and a blank one.

"Thanks." Samuel said.

"Samuel, I want you to write an letter to Mr. Jake to apologize for taking his watch."

Samuel didn't answer for a few minutes. "Okay" he said as he continued to write.

"Please bring me your game boy when your finished. You have broken commandments made by God, twice.

Samuel wrote the address on the envelope, and then inserted the letter. He sealed it and pushed it away before grabbing for his crutches.

Samuel before you go to your room, let's pray." Before Samuel could protest, Sarah stood up and put her hands on her son's shoulders. "First, Samuel I almost forgot, the man who saved your life, has asked about you often. Samuel just looked at her. "Honey, repeat after me. Lord please help me to be a better person. Show me there is not a gang who is greater than you. Help me to understand what I'm praying for. In Jesus name Amen." Samuel stood up, but kept his head down while getting his crutches and heading for his room.

After Samuel got to his room he went to the bed and sat down. How can I fit in if I was a goody goody boy. I can't he thought. Samuel picked up his game boy, and he made it back into the kitchen.

"Here," he said, handing his mother the game boy. Sarah took it. Their dinner was being warmed on the stove. Samuel sat down. Sarah looked at her son. "Samuel, here's the deal. You can get your game boy back everyday, if you want it, but you'll have to read to me for an hour. Does that sound good?"

"Even the weekends?," he asked surprised.

"Yes. We will start right after dinner today. I"m going to work tomorrow and, Miss Mary, will be here, so if you want to read to her you can." The two were silent, while they listen to music doing dinner. After dinner Sarah left the kitchen. Second later she returned with a book, which she handed to Samuel. Samuel read the title.

"Seek And Ye Shall Find?" He said frowning.

"Yes it's about children your age." Samuel began to read. An hour passed.

"You did better than I thought you could do." First I'll give your medication and then you can take your game boy into your room." Samuel looked at her and stood up.

"Go and brush your teeth first, young man!" Sarah said. She had finished with the dishes when Samuel came back to get his game boy.

"Goodnight Samuel."

Samuel whispered it back. Sarah went to the phone and dialed Miss Mary to say goodnight.

CHAPTER FOURTEEN

Gordy, woke up to the smell of bacon and coffee. After getting dressed he went into the kitchen and fixed himself a plate of food, and took it to the garden to enjoy it with Rosealee, his step mother, and dad. The beautiful flowers and their fragrances always made him feel better. The three always found interesting topics to discuss together. Gordy had shared his experience with Samuel with them. The two wanted to know how he was doing. "Well, I'm going to meet him Sunday, but he's another boy being raised by his mother. As you know some boys want to follow in their father's footsteps. Good or bad. I just hope he hasn't made up his mind to become deaf, dumb, and blind. With God's help I'll do what I can for him." The two looked at him with a knowingly look. Gordy picked up his coffee cup and took his last sip, before he got up. "Time to roll," he said. He was told to have a good and safe day.

Gordy picked up his regular customers throughout the morning. He always enjoyed sharing conversations with them. Before he knew it, it was lunch time. He picked up the Mic.. "I'm taking an hour for lunch," He said into the Mic.. He than drove to one of his favorite places. Gordy parked and got out. After he opened the truck of the cab, he took out a cooler that was filled by his father, with water and juice. His father who knew his routine, filled the cooler every Saturday.

Gordy carried the cooler to the basketball court. The boys stopped playing when they saw him.

They came smiling and sweating with hand shakes. Gordy opened the cooler. The young men knew to reach right in. "How are you guys doing?" Gordy said after he and the boys had taken swallows of the ice cold drinks. "I've got those books, The Rules of Basketball, for all you guys." He saw their excitement. "But first I'm going to shoot a few hoops."

Gordy didn't have long to play around. I"m going to get back to work for a little while, but I will be back Wednesday, as usual at 5:00. Don't forget to come to the game tomorrow.' Quite a few of the young men, were laughing and joking, and two of them carried the cooler, when they walked Gordy back to his cab. Gordy opened the truck and took out the books. "I think there's one for all of you," he said passing them out.

"Thanks man, wow, I always wanted one of these," was heard among them all.

"Hope to see you all tomorrow, and you all are welcome," Gordy said from inside the cab's window. He picked up the MIC., after he pulled out of the park. "I'm back in the cab." He felt good. Three busy hours had passed, before he picked up the MIC. again to say he was signing out. The day was still beautiful when he headed home. The radio was on low, he turned it up to complete his ride home.

Smoke was coming from the backyard, which meant, bar-b-que. Thank you Lord for this day, Gordy prayed when he pulled into the garage. He unlocked the door, laid his keys down and headed toward his room to take a shower. After he got dressed, he went and sat on the patio. He inhaled deeply. The different fragrances made him glad to be alive. After he greeted some friends and relatives, he poured himself a cold drink. He got comfortable in a lounger chair, and decided to do relaxing things for the rest of the day.

CHAPTER FIFTEEN

Sarah rose early. She got dressed and fixed breakfast. After she set the table, she went into Samuel's room and woke him up. She had to shake him serval times.

Samuel thought he was dreaming until he smelled bacon and pancakes. Sarah turned on the lights, which made him squint as he sat up in bed. "Good morning," Sarah said cheerfully.

"Good morning mom." The smell coming from the kitchen made him wish he could move faster. Lifting the covers off his legs, he shifted and moved them out of bed. His mom always looked and smelled good, but he didn't tell her that. He reached for the crutches his mother held for him. Sarah left the room when she saw her son put the last crutch under his arm. Samuel followed behind her. He saw the table from the hall. He wanted to run to it, but he couldn't. He went to the bathroom first. Ten minutes later Samuel stood smiling at the table. When the two were seated Sarah held out her hand. Samuel took her hand and the two bowed their heads. "Samuel will you please say the grace?"

Samuel looked at her, but finally bowed his head again and said grace as he was taught to say. After grace, Sarah picked up her son's medication and shook it. She picked up a spoon and gave him the medication. Before she could put the top back on the medicine bottle, she saw her son put four pancakes, and six pieces of bacon on his plate. Twenty minutes later a knock was heard at the door. "Come in Miss Mary."

Miss Mary came in and sat at the table where Sarah had placed a plate and coffee cup. Sarah got up. "I've got to go Miss Mary. You know your at home. Sarah placed her plate and cup in the sink. She picked up her purse and went back to the table and gave her son a kiss. "I'll call you later Miss Mary," she said going out the door.

"See you later," Samuel called after the door closed.

Samuel finished his breakfast, but sat at the table with Miss Mary. He picked up the remote and turned on the T.V.. He watched T.V. ,Miss Mary read the news paper and sipped her coffee. Shortly after, he took his crutches from the chair and got up. He knew Miss Mary was watching him when he walked away. He went to the bathroom to freshen up. Miss Mary was clearing the kitchen when he came out of the bathroom. Samuel went to his room and got dressed. I'm pretty good with these sticks, he said to himself going back into the kitchen.

"Miss Mary, can I go out side for some air?"

Miss Mary didn't answer him. She wiped her hands on a towel. Samuel was taken back, when she grabbed the keys and her jacket. Oh no! Samuel thought and went out the door that Miss Mary held for him. As Miss Mary locked the door, an idea came to him. "Miss Mary, can I go and see one of my friends? He lives up the street. I'll be careful."

Miss Mary smiled, and told him she'll love to meet one of his friends. The two started walking up the street. Samuel stopped. "Oh I just remembered, he won't be home today." Miss Mary laughed lightly. "What's so funny?" Samuel asked her. She shook her head from side to side. Samuel looked at her, but she continue to walk. Samuel noticed there were a lot of people outside, and he noticed Miss Mary was greeting them as if she knew them all. " Miss Mary, do you know all these people you're talking to?"

Samuel knew he had to wait a minute for the answer. she shook her head no. The two had walked farther, before she told him, that everyone was connected or related in some way. They might be a cousin, no matter what color of their skin.

He looked at Miss Mary in disbelief. This old lady must be crazy, Samuel thought. They continued to walk. Finally the two crossed the street and headed back. He felt his legs getting tired. Miss Mary asked him if he wanted to rest awhile. "Kind of" he told her. A block away was a bench. He sighed loud as he sat down and placed the crutches on the side of him. He watched Miss Mary go up the street. Soon she disappeared into one of the stores. Some minutes later, she reappeared with two large ice cream cones. Samuel took his favorite flavor when Miss Mary handed it to him. Without saying a word the two cooled and moisten their mouths with the cold, tasty ice cream. After the cones were eaten, the two remained seated for a while. Samuel reached for his crutches, when Miss Mary stood up and stretched. About twenty minutes later, they stood in front of their door. Finally Miss Mary opened the door and Samuel followed closely in. Yes!, Samuel's insides howled when Miss Mary sat two bottles of cold water on the table. He picked up a bottle, opened it, and drank most of it. He put it down and went to the bathroom. When he returned Miss Mary gave him his pills. He used the rest of his water to take the pills.

"Miss Mary, I'm going to take a nap" he called as he made his way to his bed. He was too tired to play his game. He laid down, and his mind began to think about what Miss Mary had said. No way people are that friendly. Even at school everyone had their own little group. But lately his had been the office. He just wanted to be tough and defiant. This way people would label him a bad boy. The same way they label his father. Soon Samuel was sleep.

CHAPTER SIXTEEN

Sarah looked at the time. The restaurant had been so busy she didn't take a brake. She had less than an hour before quitting time. She decided to take a break and call Mr. Mann. She found a quite place, and dialed his number.

"Hello," Gordy said

"Hello Mr. Mann, this is Sarah Willaby. How are you?" Do you have a few minutes?"

"Yes I do have time to talk to you, but will you please call me Gordy?"

"Thank you Gordy. First are you allergic to any foods?" And you can call me Sarah."

"No Sarah, none that I know of."

"That's good Gordy. I decided not to tell my son who's coming to dinner. I'll introduce you as Gordy."

"I don't think he got a good look at me. He was running, and tried to climb that fence too fast."

"If he recognizes you, that will be even better. He needs to learn a lesson, and apologize to you." Sarah then told Gordy about the watch.

"That's not showing he has learned his lesson."

"I know, I'm praying, and I'm going to take him to counseling."

"Sarah, I have a basketball game at 6:30 on Sunday. Would you and your son like to come?"

"That will put the icing on the cake. Sure I'll plan for it."

"Okay. I'll be there at 3:00."

"Fine. I'll see you tomorrow." The two hung up and Sarah went back to work.

At quitting time, Sarah said her goodnights and headed for the door. Sarah's thoughts were on Samuel and Gordy. Within half of an hour, she was home and unlocking her door. "Hello," she called from the kitchen. Miss Mary came into the kitchen. She had been reading to Samuel.

"Thank you Miss Mary, but now Samuel has to read to me. I stopped and got some submarines for dinner." She followed Miss Mary back into the living room, where Samuel was seated. Miss Mary smiled and told Sarah she had some washing to do upstairs , but she'll see her tomorrow after church. She told Samuel goodnight and said she had had a very nice day with him.

Samuel saw a pleased look on his mother's face, before she turned to walk Miss Mary to the door. Miss Mary and his mother were speaking low in the kitchen. He hoped Miss Mary didn't tell about him wanting to see his friends. Ten minutes after Sarah Closed the door behind Miss Mary, there was a knock at the door. Sarah's smile changed when she opened the door. It was one of Samuel's bad boys friends. She didn't want this boy to be with Samuel. "Hi Jr., how are you?" She asked him.

The boy mumbled, "Gilled or chilled, and asked to speak to Samuel for a minute.

Samuel had heard his voice. "Hey man! Here I come," Samuel said, as he approached the kitchen. Sarah went to the refrigerator and opened the freezer, She heard the boys whispering.

"Mom, me and JR, are going to sit outside on the stairs for a little while. Okay?"

"Okay, but don't forget about what you have to do for an hour."

"I know, I know," he told her, and went out of the door.

The two boys walked to the front of the apartment before they sat down. The evening air felt good. Before Samuel could get comfortable with his leg, and crutches, his friend JR. reached in his sock and took something out. When Jr. looked around, Samuel looked around too. His friend sneakily put a rolled marijuana into Samuel's hand.

"Thanks man, I can't smoke it now, but I will soon." His friend JR., snickered, and made his mouth come to the side. "Man," he whispered and put his hand out. Samuel gave him a high five. "That was funny. How you snatched homeboy's wallet and ran. Now that was cool. Everybody said, "That boy got heart!"

"Yea man," Samuel said laughing quietly, "If it wasn't for that fence he would never have caught me." Samuel pushed the marijuana deeper in his sock and the two laughed. JR. Stood up.

"I've got this chick waiting for me, man. She's easy man, you know what I mean. I'll see you soon." They exchanged handshakes, and JR. walked away. On his way to the door Samuel wished he could smoke what the boy had given him.

Sarah had a seven-up cake in the oven , when Samuel came back in the house. She had planned the menu for the next day. "Samuel came around the table and sat in front of the book. After he picked up the book he began reading. Sarah listened, but she wondered if any of the information was inspiring him to do better. "Do you like reading this book?" She asked her son when he was finished reading.

"Yea, it's alright."

Sarah was finished with the potatoes. She got up and put them in a pot, which she put on the stove. She opened the refrigerator and took out the pop and sub-marines. She placed these on the table, and got two glasses before she sat down. The two opened their subs. When Sarah said grace, she asked God to give her son a change of heart and mind. She looked at her son, who had not quite looked at her.

"Son I wanted you to read more, because it'll help you to read, write, and speak much better. I chose this book, SEEK AND YE SHALL FIND, because it's about children your age. These children find out about people from the past and a few of the present, who did wonderful things for this world, in spite of their pitfalls and handicaps. Just like Jesus, they will be forever remembered for their present on earth. Most of them succeeded during slavery times. Sarah began eating her sub.

"What do you think pushes a lot of people..TO DO OR DIE TRYING?" This really got her son's attention. He looked at her in dismay, before he spoke.

"You can't be afraid to die, Samuel said.

"No son, it means you do your best at what you know you're good at, or what you're learning to be good at. Those people in the book knew they could make something new or something better. It might took a long time, but they never gave up trying. They shared their presence on earth with others. That's one of the ways we love one another." The two finished their meal in silence.

When Samuel got up, he went into the bathroom. He decided to take a shower, so his mother couldn't ask him anymore questions or tell him things that had him to think differently. His shower bag, pjs, and housecoat were behind the door. After preparing his thigh, he got into the shower. The water made him feel good. He lather up, but as the water ran over him, he thought about what his mother had said. How did she know about the song. She is sort of smart, he had to admit. But...I don't know...finally he got out and toweled off. He was bare footed when he balled his clothes up placed them under his arms and grabbed one crutch and came out of the bathroom.

The cake was out of the oven and the salad made. The rest of the Sunday's dinner would be made in the morning. She had seen Samuel finally come out of the bathroom. Now it was her turn to relax in her favorite place. When she went into the bathroom her feet touched Samuel's sneakers and socks. Instantly she bent down to pick them up. "Oh my God!" She mourned. Tears instantly made her eyes blurry. She felt weak as she took a seat on the edge of the bathtub and stared at the object on the floor.

Samuel sat on his bed thinking about his friend JR. As quick as lighting he began to search the ball of clothes he had brought from the bathroom. Nervously he grabbed his crutch and stood up. And as fast as he could go he went into the bathroom. He didn't know or see until he went in. The hurt look on his mother's face told him she had found the marijuana. He froze when his mother looked at him.

"How long have you been smoking marijuana?" Sarah asked, as the tears began to flow rapidly.

"For a little while, but I don't smoke it all the time," Samuel answered in a low voice. His mind was telling him to be tough and act like so what, but he saw how this was hurting his mother. He felt like he did on the fence, scared and confused, only this time his mother was crying from the pain.

"Go back to your room." Sarah finally managed to say. A numbness had engulfed her. No wonder his personality had changed, she thought. The tub edge became uncomfortable. She got up and closed the bathroom door. Somewhat like an zombie, she picked up the marijuana and flashed it down the toilet. God, give me strength she whispered, preparing the water and her self for her bath. The water and the fragrance of the bubbles smelled and felt good. She laid back and closed her eyes. A thought came to her. God had given her the answer. Because Samuel had been smoking this drug, his personality had changed over the past year. My baby probably doesn't know any thing about marijuana. No wonder his grades had came down. He's having trouble with thinking correctly. I've got to get help for him immediately. Before she got out of the tub, she decided to write his father for help.

Samuel picked up his game, but placed it back on the desk. Toughen up, he told himself. JR. Had made him feel good. Now the boys knew he was tough. Mom is mad right now, but it always seemed like she forgot or forgave me soon. I wish I had got to smoke some of it, before she found it. He stretched out on the bed and closed his eyes. He opened them fast. When he had closed his eyes, he saw his mother's face. She was so sad with tears and frowns on her face. He felt his heart begin to beat faster as her eyes seemed to stare in his eyes.

"Samuel sit up!" Samuel jumped. His mom stood before him with a glass of water and his medication. She was still mad, but she smelled nice. Samuel began to sit up.

"Samuel if you had taken your meds and smoked that marijuana you might have flipped out. Have you ever seen a person who wasn't in their right mind?" Samuel shook his head yes, before he reached out to take the water and his medication.

"God is good. You can't see it, even though God has kept his arms around you." Sarah took her son's face in her hand. "You, young man, will be getting help soon. Monday we will be going to the library, where we will find a book on marijuana. And then I will find a rehab. Facility, to help you with your bad habits. Sarah took the glass out of Samuel's hand. I know where JR. lives, so I will be paying his parents a visit."

"No mom!, please don't. He wont like me anymore!" Samuel's face was in a raged. "But I will! With the love I have for you, you won't need him." Sarah watched her not quite thirteen son, turn his face away from her. She stood for a few more minutes looking at his back, and then around his room.

"One day, you'll thank me for what we're about to do." Sarah took a deep breath and turned off the light before she exit the room.

Chapter Seventeen

Gordy woke early Sunday morning to the smell of coffee and biscuits. Because of his dinner date, he decided to get started earlier, and drive for half a day. After having breakfast, he said, "See you two later." Getting into the cab, he started the ignition, and reached for the Mic. "Good morning Fred, I'm ready and able." he said to the dispatcher. He replaced the mic.,and backed out of the driveway. A signal on the mic, let Gordy know he was heard.

As usual, time flew by fast. His passengers had made his day pleasant. At 12:15, he had one more passenger to pick up and transport to his destination. The elderly man stood in front of his house. He was smiling when he got into the cab. This man not only dressed very well, but his personality and wisdow was overwhelming. "Good morning Mr. Ace." The man's smile spoke for him. Gordy know where to take him.

Twenty minutes later they arrived. "Here we are Mr. Ace. That'll be $3.00." The man leaned forward and handy Gordy $3.00, and an envelope. "Thank you." the two said at the same time. Gordy placed both items on the seat, got out and opened the door for Mr. Ace. Gordy waited until Mr. Ace made his entrance, before getting back into the cab.

On his way home Gordy prayed that all would go well with Sarah and her son.

It didn't take long before Gordy was pulling into his driveway. Before he got out, he picked up the envelope and opened it. It read: Dear Mr. Mann, this question was asked of me...If you only had one day to live, how would you live it? I will live my by remembering the smiles of others. Thank you for yours. Ace. Gordy turned it over. There was a picture of Mr. Ace smiling, he smiled back. He placed Mr. Ace's smiling face on the sun visor and got out of the cab.

CHAPTER EIGHTEEN

Sarah was busy cooking and cleaning, when Samuel came into the kitchen.

"Good morning MY son," Sarah opened the oven and pulled out the Cornish hens to check them. After placing them back, she went into the living room. Samuel looked around. It looked like his mother had been cooking and cleaning all night. He wanted to ask if they were having company, but he didn't. Cereal bowls and cereal were on the table. Samuel went to the refrigerator and got the milk.

"We're having a guest for dinner, so I want you to take your shower early, and be ready by 2:00." Samuel heard his mother say from the living room. He began to fix his cereal without answering. He sat down and ate while reading the cereal box. His mother appeared at the kitchen door, just when he was ready to get up. "Stay put, I want you to read to me while I finish preparing dinner."

His mind told him to tell her, he didn't feel like it, but his heart allowed him to take the book she handed him. But he did use his mean puffed up face as he read.

Sarah watched her son's put on face. She knew in her heart that he cared and loved her. She couldn't believe the children who disrespected their parents, but who would never allow another child or anyone else to do the same. Sarah refused to get upset, because Samuel had been trying to become who he wasn't for a while.

After he had finished reading she gave him some juice. "Thank you." was said, in a low voice.

"Your welcome. Sam, I notice that you are doing very well with your crutch and cast. That shows me , your getting better. Sarah stood up. "Will you please clear off the table, and take out the garbage. After that you can change your sheets. If you need help with anything, just holler and I'll be there." Sarah left the kitchen.

Samuel finished his juice and got up from the table. Samuel went straight to his room. The clean sheets were placed at the head of his bed. Samuel went and sat on his bed and picked up his game boy.

"Samuel make your bed, so I can mop in there." his mother said from the kitchen. Samuel began to prepare the bed for the clean sheets.

By 1:30, Sarah had finished cleaning and cooking. Samuel was in the bathroom. Sarah began to set the table. Samuel came to the kitchen door.

"Samuel, if you won't pull your pants up and don't wear your belt, you will have to wear suspenders." Sarah put her hands on her hips.

"I can't find my belt." Samuel said. Sarah had a plan, but for now she had to get ready.

"We'll talk about it later," she said and walked away. Samuel went into the living room with his game boy. A few minutes later Samuel heard a knock at the back door. He knew it was Miss Mary, as he went to opened it. "Hi Miss Mary," Samuel said and stepped aside to let her in. Miss Mary looked at him, as he tried to pull his pants up. Miss Mary went into the living room and picked up the Sunday's paper and sat down. When she saw Sarah come out of the bathroom, she asked if there was anything that she could help with.

"No, Miss Mary, thank you. You look nice." Sarah walked into her bedroom. I'll be out in a few," she told Miss Mary, before she closed the door. Miss Mary handed Samuel, who had sat across from her the funnies and sport pages from the paper. Samuel placed the sports paper on his lap and began to read the funnies.

Sarah came out of the bathroom, and went directly to the kitchen. As she began to warm the food, she thought, what if Samuel does remember Gordy?

Gordy had told her, Samuel was unconscious before he put him in his arms. She dismissed the thought as she stirred the pots. The front door bell rang. Sarah went to the door.

CHAPTER NINETEEN

"Hello Gordy, how are you?" Sarah said smiling

"Blessed," Gordy said, handing her a grocery bag. Sarah took the bag. "Please come in."

"I brought some cold apple juice, if that's alright."

"It's right on time. Thank you. Sarah closed the door. Gordy this is my son Samuel." Sarah watched her son's face as Gordy walked over to Samuel and extended his hand. The two shook hands. Sarah went to Miss Mary, and put her arms around her shoulders. "Gordy, this is my friend and neighbor, Miss Mary." Gordy went over and took both of Miss Mary's hands in his.

"It's always nice to meet someone who knows how to be a friend," Gordy said smiling.

Miss Mary smiled and glanced at Samuel.

"Gordy please have a seat. Dinner will be ready in a few minutes. Miss Mary, will you come in the kitchen with me please?"

Miss Mary got up and followed Sarah.

I know my mother probably called this man because of what she found in the bathroom, Samuel told himself, eying Gordy. He's trying to fool me by dressing like a basketball coach. Oh!, maybe he is one, I see a whistle around his neck. His team must were black and gold. When Gordy came and sat where Miss Mary had sat, Samuel pretended he was reading the funnies.

Gordy knew Samuel had checked him out, but he had showed no signs of knowing him.

"How did you hurt your leg?" he asked Samuel.

Samuel felt his face getting warm. "I had an accident," I had an accident," he told Gordy, squirming with the paper.

"Do you play basketball?" Gordy asked.

"No. I play football." Samuel held the paper in one hand and looked at Gordy.

"What position?" Gordy looked in Samuel eyes.

"I'm learning to play different positions."

"That's good! That way you'll find out what you can do best. Have you ever played basketball?"

"I used to"

"I'm a coach for St. John's church, Samuel. I have a game today at 5:30. Would you like to come to it? You can be my guest and sit at the table with me."

Samuel thought quick. This would be a way to get out of the house. "Yea!"

"Okay. Your mom can come along too." Before Samuel could say anything else, Sarah came in and told them dinner was ready. Gordy waited for Samuel to get up and walk in front of him. Miss Mary and Sarah sat at the heads of the table. Samuel and Gordy sat across from one another.

"Gordy, will you please say grace?" Sarah asked.

Heads were bowed. Gordy proceeded. "Because you have been so gracious to share your food and time with me, I would like to share what my father shared with me." Everyone's eyes looked at Gordy. We all have to learn, in one way or another, that none of us get seconds in this world. We all get new chances till the end of our lives. But not second chances in the same circumstances. And the great difference between one person and other is how one takes hold of, and uses their first chance. Also how one takes their fall, if it is scored against them. Lord bless these people and this food. Amen."

Sarah and Miss Mary's eye's were watery, and Samuel looked dazed.

"These are some of my favorite foods, Sarah. Gordy said, as he reached for a Cornish hen.

"Please help yourself." Sarah told Gordy.

"Samuel has agreed to come to my game today at 5:30. I'll like to show you some other boys Samuel's age, who are doing great in the game, Sarah. Of course, Gordy held up his glass to Miss Mary. "you are welcome to come."

Miss Mary, toasted back, thanked him, and said, she'll take a rain check.

Gordy wiped his mouth. "I start picking up some of my players at 5:00.

I Brought my van, so there will be enough room."

"That's fine. We'll prepare to leave right after dinner," Sarah said. By 4:30, dinner and the dishes were completed. Miss Mary, thanked Sarah and told them to have fun, before she left. Gordy noticed, it wasn't Samuel's cast that was slowing him down, it was his beltless pants. He remembered how Samuel was running and holding his pants up that day. Today it was funny. Minutes later, the three, were on their way to pick up Gordy's team members.

Samuel didn't know any of the boys, Gordy picked up. They all gave him and Gordy firm handshakes. They called his mom, Miss Willaby, when introduced. Samuel noticed something different between, Gordy and his team players. Softness! Yea, Samuel said to himself. They were excited and happy. He was too, but he knew not to show it. Gordy pulled into a parking lot and parked. He pushed a button and the rear end opened. Everyone except him got out. Gordy and the boys went to the back of the van. Within seconds Gordy returned with Samuel's crutch, and helped Samuel out, while the boys unloaded the back.

Sarah stepped aside to let Samuel continue to walk by him self. She almost laughed as she watched her son, struggle with his pants and crutch. Finally everyone was in, and Samuel sat next to Gordy. Samuel viewed more of the team's togetherness with one another as they prepared themselves for the game. Gordy blew his whistle. Everyone stood up except Samuel. He saw how the teams joined hand and heard a strong pledge to themselves and thanks to God.

A boy came to the table with water. He handed Samuel and Sarah one, and placed one on the table. The game had started. To Samuel it was good, but boring. He was used to seeing disagreements, rudeness, and fights. At half time Gordy approached the table.

"How do you like my team's plays?", he asked Samuel.

"Samuel shrugged his shoulders. "They're Okay."

"Okay?"

"They need to be a little faster," Samuel told Gordy.

"Maybe you can work with me at the next practice game." Gordy opened his water and drank most of it.

"Is it a good game?" Gordy asked him.

"Yea," was all Samuel said.

Gordy smiled and stood up. He patted Samuel on the shoulder and went closer to the game.

When Gordy's team won, Samuel cheered too. He also laughed with everyone else at the video afterwards. When Gordy had taken his team home, he asked Samuel what he knew about basketball.

"I've got some moves," Samuel said in a low voice.

"No son, I asked you what do you know about basketball."

"One team has got to get more points, and not let the other team make their baskets." Samuel smiled a little, he knew he knew that.

"Son, if you want to work with me, you've got to know a lot more about the game of basketball. I'll help you. But if you don't want to know information about things you enjoy doing or something you want to do, than I can't help you.

Samuel remained quiet. Soon Gordy pulled up in front of their house.

"Samuel, I've got a basketball book you can read, if you want to. It'll give us something to talk about when I call you tomorrow. Gordy had an extra book in his glove compartment, which he took out and gave it to Samuel.

"Thank you," Samuel said. Because of his beltless pants, he put the book in his back pocket.

"Thank you Gordy, It was very enjoyable." Sarah said.

"Both of you are welcome, I'll call about 6:00, tomorrow."

"Okay," the two said, as Gordy got back in the van.

CHAPTER TWENTY

The next day Sarah began to search the yellow pages for the Rehabilitation Center for children. By 10:30, she had gotten an appointment for Samuel. At 12:30, Sarah and Samuel walked in the building. Samuel was nervous. He was glad his boys were in school, because he had a belt on. A lady behind a desk asked Samuel his name. She then told them to have a seat. A few minutes later, a man in a stylist suit came and introduced himself as Joe Davis. When he gave Sarah some papers to fill out, he told her, he wanted to get acquainted with Samuel, while she filled them out.

Samuel followed Joe, which he said for him to call him. "Are you scared to be yourself?," Joe asked Samuel, after they were seated.

Samuel looked at the man in disbelief.

"I asked you that because so many boys your age are. Do you know why?"

Samuel shook his head no.

"Because they are too young to know who they are. But thank god no two people are alike. I know you don't know me, but I had to find out who I was to. Smoking marijuana will only confuse you. Do you like to read?"

"Yes sometimes." Samuel said.

"Good! Read this please. Samuel took the small book, but the letters were big. "Important things to know about marijuana.   Most teenagers don't use marijuana, because this stuff can mess up your performance in school, sports, parties, and at home. Your have trouble with thinking and problem solving. It can lead to risky sexual behavior, resulting in exposure to sexually transmitted diseases.

"You read well. Stop getting high. Take vitamins if you want to feel good. Here's my number. I got yours. If your in a gang, get out now! Gang brings pain. I'll help you. Any question? Joe stared hard.

"No." Samuel said nervously.

"Relax, and find out who you are. We all have our own gifts. It takes time. It will come and you too can make a good contribution to this world. Keep busy! I'm not far away. See you next week." The two walked back to Sarah.

Sarah handed him the papers. "I'll call you tomorrow Ms. Willaby." He said, turned and walked back to his office. Sarah smiled, and thanked God, silently as she and her son left the building.

When they returned home, Sarah was surprised to see a letter from Samuel's father. She did give Samuel's letter to the mail man, the following day.

She gave the letter to Samuel to read. He read it out loud;

"Dear son, please forgive me for my role of not being the father, or man I should have been. Instead of being proud, that I was blessed to be born, I became rebellious. I began to blame others for the deaf, dumb, and blind things I did. Sure I knew better, I knew right from wrong, but when you never find out who you really are, you become lost in the sauce that doesn't smell too good. Son please stay in school, go to college or take a trade. There's a time and place for everyone, if you can't find it, than your place and time will be here, ONE STEP IN HELL. Promise me, you won't give your head to drugs or alcohol. Fill your head up with important issues and details of life, so you'll be able to pass it on to your family or friends. These words were told to me many years ago, only now do I have time to hear. I should have lived and shared them a long time ago. Son respect yourself and others.

Tell your mother I'm sorry for not respecting her. Always remember son, females deserve respect everyday, they are our life support. P.S., I received your letter, Please remember to respect adults. Love always, your father."

Sarah heard her son's voice tremble. His hands shook a little. His eyes were watery when he looked at her. "Mom I'm tried, I'm going to lay down."

"Okay baby." Sarah watched her son go to his room, and she had a feeling that when he came out, he would be a better person. "God is good, she whispered, her eyes also were watery.

Samuel picked up his letter from his father, when he woke up. He read it again. It made him feel different. His eyes went to the book Gordy had given him. He picked it up. The first page's title was, DO YOU WANT TO BECOME A GOOD BASKETBALL PLAYER. You must have the right attitude toward life.

Sarah couldn't believe her eyes, when she peeked in Samuel's door and saw him reading the basketball book. She silently and quickly left the door.

At 6:00, the phone rung. " Samuel, telephone," Sarah handed her son the phone. Samuel smiled, he knew who it was.

"Hi Gordy."

"Hi Samuel, how are you feeling?"

"Good, I read a few pages of the book you give me."

"That's great! If it's alright with your mother, how about if I come and pick you up in about twenty minutes. We can ride to the court where quite a few of my friends practice. Will you please put your mother on the phone?"

"Gordy wants to take to you," Samuel spoke so excited, it sounded like he was out of breath.

"Hello Gordy,"

"Hi Sarah, how are you?"

"I almost feel like shouting, she laughed.

"Well that sounds good! he laughs too.

"Sarah, would you mind if I come and pick Samuel up in about twenty minutes? I believe I should tell him about who I am today.

"No, I don't mind, and I think that is a good thing to do today too."

When Gordy rung the doorbell, Sarah and Samuel came to the door. Sarah had sparkles in her eyes, when she greeted him.

"We'll be back in a couple of hours."

"Okay."

The two didn't speak until Gordy made the turn into the park and he parked. He turned to speak.

"Samuel, I do want us to be friends, but before we can become friends, I need to be completely honest with you. First do you like to be called Sam or Samuel.

Samuel looked at him with wide eyes. "Sam"

"Sam, my name is Gordy Mann. I'm the man that chased you, and then saved your life." The two looked at one another.

"Maybe I should have told you who I was Sunday, but I guess God, didn't want it that way." I forgave you, so you can forgive yourself. Our hands are not made to get us in trouble. They were made to keep us out of trouble, because what you do with them has to please God and you. Do you still want to work with me?"

"I can't believe you want to be My friend. Yes, I want to work with you." The two shook hands, got out and walked to the court. All of a sudden, the two were surrounded. "This is my new friend, Sam. He's going to help me with the plays and growth of my team." Samuel got a lot of hand shakes and encouragements. Someone threw Gordy the ball, and Gordy made some shots. After Gordy said his good bys, and the two were back in the car. He asked Samuel if he had a ball.

"No I don't"

Gordy pushed a button, got out of the car, and lift the truck open When he got back in he handed Samuel a ball. There was writings on it. Samuel read It. A NEW DAY, A NEW BEGINNING. The two looked at one another for the first time.